W9-BWU-434

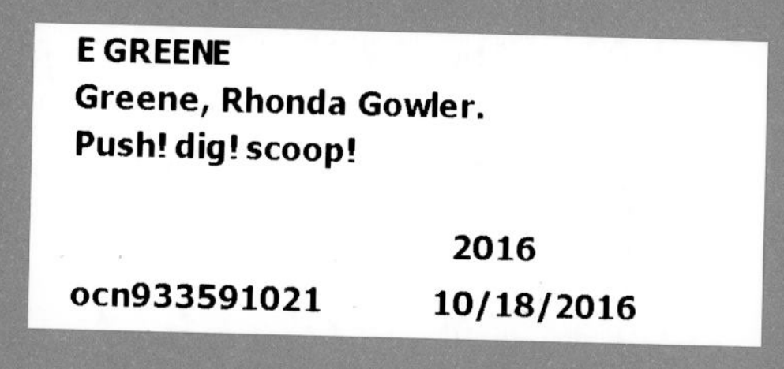
E GREENE
Greene, Rhonda Gowler.
Push! dig! scoop!
2016
ocn933591021
10/18/2016

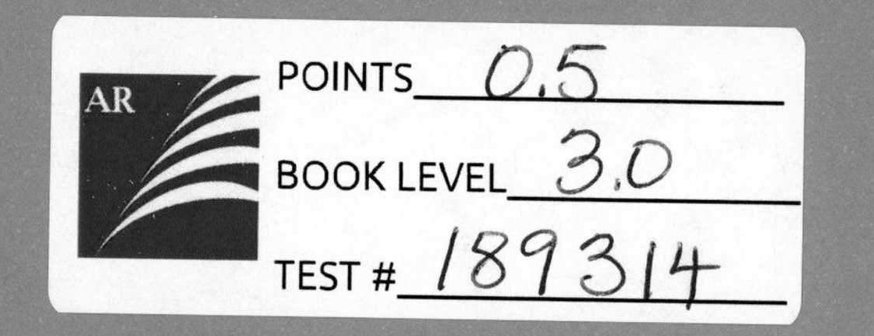
AR
POINTS 0.5
BOOK LEVEL 3.0
TEST # 189314

PUSH! DIG! SCOOP!

A Construction Counting Rhyme

Rhonda Gowler Greene
illustrated by Daniel Kirk

BLOOMSBURY
NEW YORK LONDON OXFORD NEW DELHI SYDNEY

First published in the United States of America in October 2016 by Bloomsbury Children's Books
www.bloomsbury.com

Bloomsbury is a registered trademark of Bloomsbury Publishing Plc

For information about permission to reproduce selections from this book, write to Permissions, Bloomsbury Children's Books, 1385 Broadway, New York, New York 10018
Bloomsbury books may be purchased for business or promotional use. For information on bulk purchases please contact
Macmillan Corporate and Premium Sales Department at specialmarkets@macmillan.com

Library of Congress Cataloging-in-Publication Data
Names: Greene, Rhonda Gowler. | Kirk, Daniel, illustrator.
Title: Push! dig! scoop! : a construction counting rhyme /
by Rhonda Gowler Greene ; illustrated by Daniel Kirk.
Description: New York : Bloomsbury, 2016.
Summary: In this variation on the classic song "Over in the Meadow," mother and father trucks show their youngsters how to build down at the construction site, from "mama bulldozer with her little dozer one" to "mama steamroller with her little rollers ten."
Identifiers: LCCN 2015040013
ISBN 978-0-8027-3506-5 (hardcover) • ISBN 978-1-68119-086-0 (e-book) • ISBN 978-1-68119-087-7 (e-PDF)
Subjects: | CYAC: Stories in rhyme. | Trucks—Fiction. | Construction equipment—Fiction. | Counting. | BISAC: JUVENILE FICTION/Transportation/Cars & Trucks. | JUVENILE FICTION/Bedtime & Dreams. | JUVENILE FICTION/Concepts/Counting & Numbers.
Classification: LCC PZ8.3.G824 Pu 2016 | DDC [E]—dc23
LC record available at http://lccn.loc.gov/2015040013

Art created with black ink drawings on paper, with colors and texture added digitally • Typeset in Autoradiographic • Book design by John Candell
Printed in China by Leo Paper Products, Heshan, Guangdong
2 4 6 8 10 9 7 5 3 1

All papers used by Bloomsbury Publishing, Inc., are natural, recyclable products made from wood grown in well-managed forests. The manufacturing processes conform to the environmental regulations of the country of origin.

For my book buddies,

Julian, Mackenzie, and Adeleine. We "dig" books!

—R. G. G.

For Ethan

—D. K.

Over by the dirt pile in the sizzling summer sun
works a mama bulldozer with her little dozer **ONE**.

“Push!” says the mama. “I push!” says the one.
So they push oosh oosh in the sizzling summer sun.

Over by the dirt pile—what a tough and burly crew!—
works a papa excavator with his excavators **TWO**.

"Dig!" says the papa. "We dig!" say the two.
So they dig *schlup schlup*. What a tough and burly crew!

Over by the dirt pile, just as mighty as can be,
works a papa wheel loader with his little loaders **THREE**.

“Scoop!” says the papa. “We scoop!” say the three.

So they scoop sloop sloop, just as mighty as can be.

Over by the dirt pile, tipping loads all set to pour,
works a mama dump truck with her little dumpers **FOUR**.

"Spill!" says the mama. "We spill!" say the four.
So they spill plomp plomp. Now they're ready for some more!

Over by the dirt pile where big beams of steel arrive
works a papa pipe layer with his little pipers **FIVE**.

"Lay!" says the papa. "We lay!" say the five.
So they lay plunk plunk where big beams of steel arrive.

Over by the dirt pile near a stack of brawny bricks
works a mama cement mixer with her little mixers **SIX**.

"Spin!" says the mama. "We spin!" say the six.

So they spin *chwurl chwurl* near a stack of brawny bricks.

Over by the dirt pile, soaring skyward up to heaven,
works a tall mama crane with her little cranes **SEVEN**.

"Lift!" says the mama.
"We lift!" say the seven.

So they lift s-s-swoop s-s-swup,
soaring skyward up to heaven.

Over by the dirt pile near the wide construction gate
works a strong papa grader with his little graders **EIGHT**.

"Scrape!" says the papa. "We scrape!" say the eight.
So they scrape scritch scratch near the wide construction gate.

Over by the dirt pile in a long and hefty line
works a papa asphalt paver with his little pavers **NINE**.

“Glide!” says the papa. “We glide!” say the nine.

So they glide **oooZ oooZ** in a long and hefty line.

Over by the dirt pile, wearing such a toothy grin,
works a mama steamroller with her little rollers **TEN**.
10

"Mash!" says the mama. "We mash!" say the ten.
So they mash *moosh moosh*, wearing such big toothy grins.

Over by the dirt pile
in the sinking summer sun,
those trucks all give a shout—
TOOT! TOOT!—
for their hard-work day is done.

Soon it's time to snooze.

They scrubble up, then snuggle in.

All listen to truck lullabies
as lights blink-wink and dim.

The moon glows cozy-bright
as they whisper, “Nighty-night.”

Then—they dream about tomorrow
at the big construction site. Shhh . . .